This book belongs to

_____

_____

D1433113

This edition published by Parragon Books Ltd in 2016

Parragon Books Ltd
Chartist House
15–17 Trim Street
Bath BA1 1HA, UK
www.parragon.com

Copyright © 2016 Disney Enterprises, Inc.

Adapted by Samantha Crockford   Designed by James Burlinson & Vanessa Mee
Illustrated by the Disney Storybook Artists   Production by Charlene Vaughan

All rights reserved. No part of this publication may be reproduced, stored in a retrieval system
or transmitted, in any form or by any means, electronic, mechanical, photocopying, recording
or otherwise, without the prior permission of the copyright holder.

ISBN 978-1-4748-5297-5

Printed in China

DISNEY MOVIE COLLECTION
A SPECIAL DISNEY STORYBOOK SERIES

DISNEY
M⊚ANA

PaRragon
Bath · New York · Cologne · Melbourne · Delhi
Hong Kong · Shenzhen · Singapore

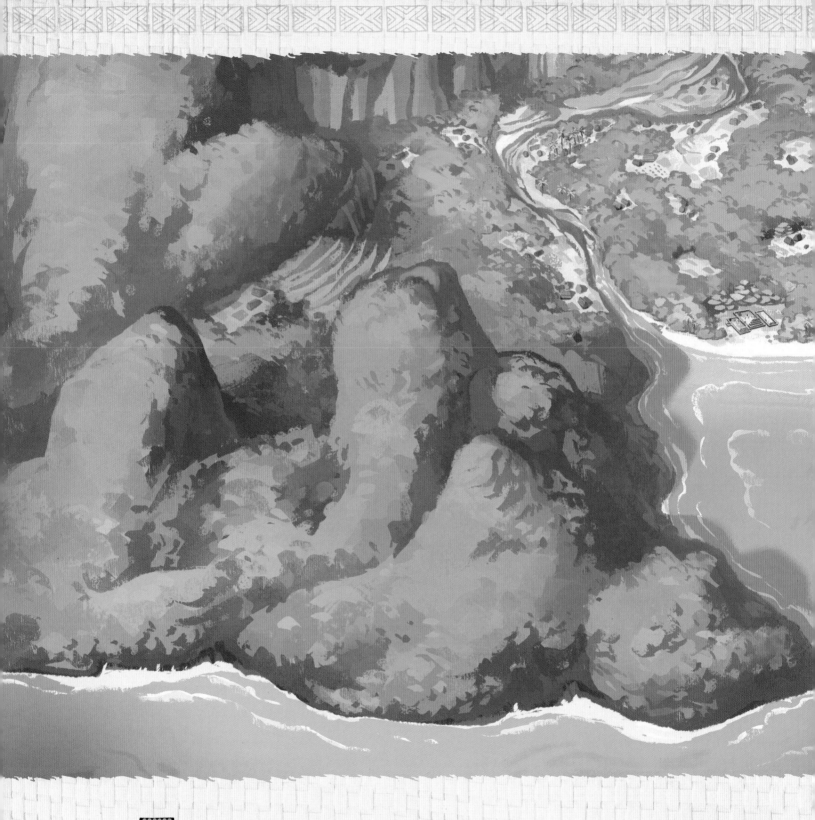

Moana was a little girl who lived with her family on the island of Motunui. Her home was a beautiful place, surrounded by a coral reef and shimmering blue seas. Her father, Tui, was chief of the island. Moana was destined to be chief too, one day.

Chief Tui cared very much about his people and made sure they were happy and safe. He didn't allow anyone to sail out beyond the coral reef, where it might be dangerous. After all, Motunui had everything the villagers needed. Who would want to leave?

Moana's grandmother, Gramma Tala, liked to tell ancient tales to the children in the village. The other toddlers would sometimes become frightened, but Moana loved the stories.

"In the beginning," Gramma Tala said, "there was only ocean, until an island emerged – the mother island, Te Fiti. Her heart had the power to create life itself, and she shared it with the world."

Gramma explained that some people wanted to take the heart and keep its power for themselves. One day, a demigod called Maui succeeded. He used his magical fishhook to steal the heart and Te Fiti began to crumble. As Maui made off, he was confronted by a monster called Te Kā. The pair fought and the heart was dropped – lost in the sea.

Not long afterwards, Moana was playing on the beach – her favourite place. She stepped out into the water and, amazingly, it rose up around her, creating a path out to sea.

Moana followed the path and spotted a little spiral stone in the water. She reached out and grasped it.

Just then, Chief Tui came looking for his daughter. The sea quickly whisked Moana back to the shore.

The toddler dropped the spiral stone on the sand as her father, and her mother Sina, took her back to the village.

Moana would have spent every day by the sea if she could, dreaming of adventures on the waves. But her parents taught her that she belonged in the village with her people.

The years passed and Moana was very happy growing up in Motunui. She learned from the people around her and, in return, helped them in any way she could.

When Moana was 16 years old, Tui took her to a
large pile of stones atop the island's highest mountain.

"One day, you will add your stone to this mountain,"
he said, "and raise our whole mountain higher."

Tui told Moana how important it was for her to stay
in the village and lead her people. Moana nodded at
her father, even though she still felt drawn to the sea.
She wanted to make him proud.

Later that day, Gramma Tala found Moana and led her along
a rocky path to the furthest point of their island, to a secret cave.

"What's in there?" Moana asked.

"The answer," Gramma Tala replied, "to the question you
keep asking yourself. 'Who are you meant to be?'"

Moana climbed inside the cave and gasped in amazement at what she saw. The huge cave was filled with sailing boats! Moana began beating a big drum on one of the boats and something magical happened. In her mind, she could see her people's history. They had been great voyagers!

Moana leaped out of the cave with excitement. She asked
her grandmother why their people had stopped voyaging.
    Gramma Tala explained that after Maui took the heart of
Te Fiti, a darkness spread across the seas. The ancient chiefs
had stopped Moana's people from sailing to keep them safe.

Gramma Tala said that the darkness was starting to infect their island, too. Their home was in danger – unless someone found Maui and took him to restore the heart of Te Fiti.

Gramma took a spiral stone from her necklace. It was the one that Moana had found in the sea when she was little. It was the heart of Te Fiti!

"The ocean chose you," Gramma told Moana.

Now that Moana knew the truth, she wanted to help save the island. She ran to the village leaders.

"We were voyagers," she cried, "we can voyage again!"

But Chief Tui quickly pulled Moana aside. He didn't believe that the spiral stone was the heart of Te Fiti and he wanted his people to stay safe on the island.

Tui threw the sprial stone to the ground. As Moana
picked it up, she spotted something that made her stop
in her tracks – it was Gramma Tala's walking stick.
But where was Gramma Tala? Something wasn't right.

Moana raced to Gramma Tala's home and found her very sick in bed. She rushed to her side.

"Go," Gramma said, in a weak voice. "You must. The ocean chose you."

"I can't leave you!" Moana protested.

"There is nowhere you could go that I won't be with you," Gramma replied.

She gave Moana the necklace to hold the heart of Te Fiti, and with the last of her strength, whispered: "Go."

Moana knew what she had to do. She packed some supplies, took a small boat from the secret cave and set sail. In the night sky she saw stars in the shape of the fishhook that Maui carried. Moana tried her best to head in that direction.

But soon, a storm rose up. WHAM! A giant wave crashed into her boat and everything faded to black.

Moana slowly opened her eyes as the sea splashed her face.
She had been washed up on the beach of a strange island.
As she looked around, she spotted tiny marks in the shape
of a giant fishhook carved into a nearby rock, and some giant
footprints in the sand.

This must be Maui's island! Moana realized in amazement.
Could the sea have brought her here?

Suddenly, Maui himself appeared! Moana summoned all her courage and told him that he must go with her to restore the heart of Te Fiti, but Maui refused. He said he had taken the heart for the humans, just as he had brought them the sun, fire and tides. All he wanted was to get his magical fishhook back, which he'd lost in his battle with Te Kā all those years ago.

Maui boasted to Moana about all the amazing feats he had achieved. But as he talked, he trapped Moana inside a cave!

Maui had been stuck on this island without his fishhook, which had the power to help him shape-shift into different animals. Now he finally had a way to leave. He went back down to the beach, boarded Moana's boat and set sail.

But Moana wasn't ready to give up on her mission. She found a way out of the cave and dived into the water. Amazingly, the sea pushed her through the water and lifted her on to her boat. Maui was surprised to see her!

"You will put back the heart!" Moana told Maui in her
bravest voice, holding the spiral-stone heart towards him.
But Maui still refused to help.

Just then, spears started landing around Moana and Maui. They were being attacked by Kakamora – tiny bandits dressed in coconut armour!

Moana batted them with her oar
and was able to keep them from
stealing the heart! Finally, together,
the pair managed to escape from the
Kakamora and sail away.

After that, Maui finally agreed to go with Moana to Te Fiti.
But they needed to fetch his fishhook first.

"We go east," said Maui, "to the lair of Tamatoa."

Maui was certain the monster Tamatoa had his hook.

"Teach me to sail," said Moana.

Maui refused at first, but then the sea knocked him over
with a poisoned dart. He couldn't move!

As he lay on the deck, Maui was forced to teach Moana all he knew. He explained that what he did was called 'wayfinding', not sailing. It meant using the sun, stars, moon, wind, waves and the currents to help you get where you want to go. Moana slowly but surely learned how it worked.

Tamatoa's lair was in Lalotai, the realm of monsters. By the next morning, the pair had reached the tall, rocky island that was the entrance to the realm. They climbed upwards until they reached a deep, dark opening.

Lalotai was underneath the sea – Moana and Maui had to pass all the way down through the water to reach it. They each took a deep breath and jumped into the pitch-black hole.

Maui landed safely, but Moana was caught by
the tongue of a huge monster! Luckily, an even
bigger monster ate the first monster, and Moana
dropped to the floor, unharmed.

After that, Moana couldn't find
Maui anywhere. She saw a cave and
bravely went inside alone. She spotted
the fishhook amongst a huge pile of
shiny gold objects. But just then, the
ground rose up to reveal ... Tamatoa!

As the monster grasped Moana in
its huge claw, Maui leaped on to the
scene and grabbed his hook.

Maui tried to shape-shift, but his
powers weren't working properly.
Tamatoa dropped Moana and started
to attack Maui!

Thinking quickly, Moana took the stone from her necklace and held it out to Tamatoa. The monster, who couldn't resist new treasures, chased Moana as she led him away from Maui. As she ran, she tripped and dropped the stone.

Moana called out to Maui: "We gotta go!"

"But – the heart!" cried Maui.

"He can have it, I've got this one," Moana replied.

She opened her hand to reveal the real heart of Te Fiti. She had used an ordinary stone to trick Tamatoa!

Before the monster had a chance to attack again, a geyser exploded underneath Moana and Maui, launching them safely through the top of the realm. They made it out alive!

Back on the boat, Moana helped Maui practise shape-shifting until he
could do it easily again. As the pair sailed towards Te Fiti, Maui told Moana
that he was born human, but his parents didn't want him. The gods gave him
the fishhook and he used it to give islands, fire and tides to the humans, but
it was never enough for them. Moana realized that Maui had taken the heart
of Te Fiti for his people, to prove his worth.

Just as the pair spotted Te Fiti in the distance, Te Kā appeared. Maui had to get past the lava monster. He turned into a huge hawk and took to the skies, clutching the heart in his claw. But Maui was no match for Te Kā, who quickly knocked him out of the sky. Moana helped Maui back on to the boat and the pair headed further towards Te Fiti. Then they watched in horror as Te Kā brought a fist of fire down towards the boat....

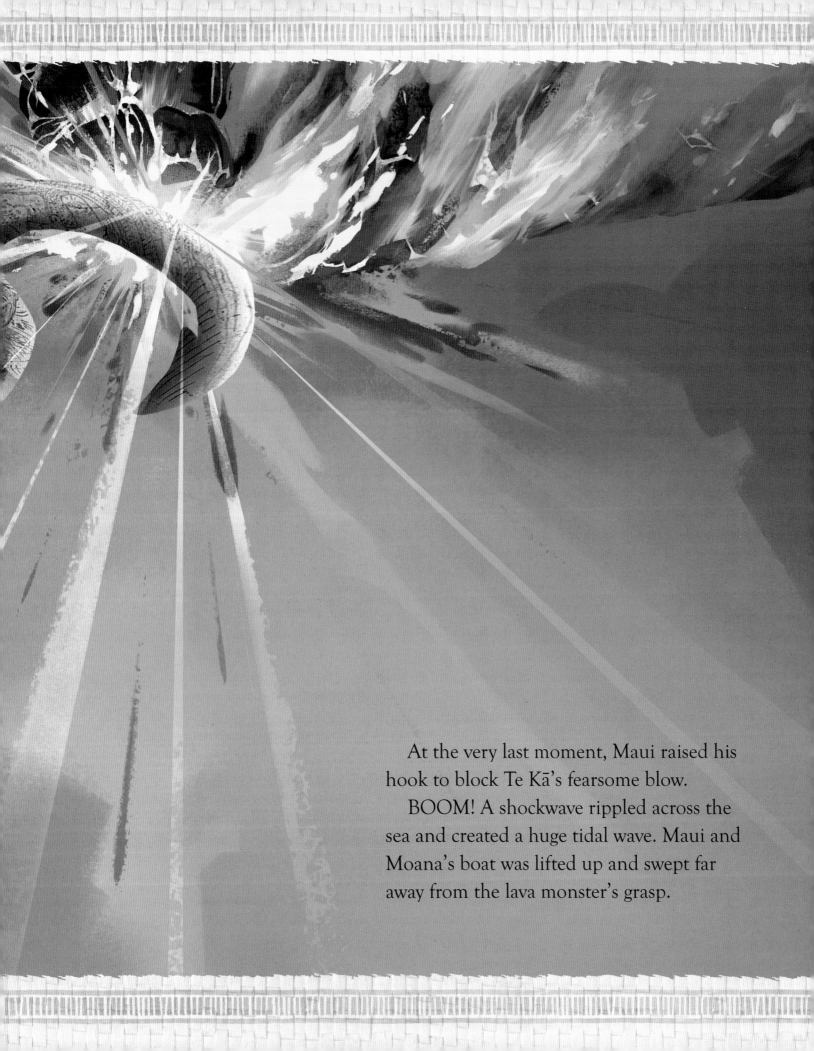

At the very last moment, Maui raised his hook to block Te Kā's fearsome blow.

BOOM! A shockwave rippled across the sea and created a huge tidal wave. Maui and Moana's boat was lifted up and swept far away from the lava monster's grasp.

The friends were now a long way from Te Fiti and their boat was in a bad way. Moana wanted to head straight back to battle Te Kā again, but then gasped as she saw that Te Kā's blow had left a huge crack in Maui's hook. "Without my hook I am nothing," Maui said.

Maui was mad at Moana. He angrily told her that the
ocean shouldn't have chosen her for this task. He dropped
the heart of Te Fiti on to the deck and used all the power
he could muster to shape-shift into a hawk. Moana tried to
convince him to stay, but he refused. He flew off into the sky.

Moana was heartbroken. She looked out across the water
and spoke to the sea with tears in her eyes.

"You chose the wrong person," she said. "You'll have to
choose somebody else."

Then she held the heart of Te Fiti out to the sea. After a
moment, the water took it from her and back below the waves.

Moana was stunned. She had
thought the sea might force her
to keep the heart and carry on.
But now, she had nothing.

Moana felt so alone. But just then, she looked into the water and saw a magnificent glowing manta ray swimming beneath her boat. Suddenly, she heard Gramma Tala's voice and looked up to see her grandmother's spirit sitting next to her. Moana was so happy!

Tala told Moana that she would stay by her side, whether she decided to go home or carry on.

As they talked, hundreds of ghostly canoes emerged around the boat. They were Moana's ancestors.
Gramma Tala asked, "Do you know who you are?"

Moana realized that this task
had always been her destiny and she
must complete it. She dived over the
side of the boat and swam deeper
and deeper into the sea. The heart
of Te Fiti glowed brightly and Moana
retrieved it from the seabed.

Moana repaired her boat as well as
she could, then set on course towards
Te Fiti once again.

Te Kā was still determined to stop Moana and hurled huge masses of molten lava at her. The monster raised its fist, but just before it struck Moana ...

... Maui appeared out of nowhere to take the blow! He had
returned. Even though his hook was broken, Maui bravely fought
Te Kā, allowing Moana to sail onwards.

When Moana reached
Te Fiti, she gasped. The island
wasn't there! It was just an
empty crater and there was no
goddess to be seen. There was
nowhere to put back the heart.

But Moana didn't panic.
She took a deep breath and
looked at Te Kā, towering over
Maui. Suddenly, she noticed
a glowing lava spiral on the
monster's chest. Moana looked
at the spiral-stone heart in her
hand. She knew what to do!

She stepped into the sea and
the water parted, creating
a huge pathway between
Moana and Te Kā.

"Moana!" Maui cried out.
"What are you doing?"

Te Kā swooped down and came to a stop in front of Moana. The monster no longer seemed frightening. In fact, Moana thought she could see a sadness behind its eyes.

Moana reached out and placed the heart into Te Kā's chest. The glow from the heart slowly began to spread across the monster's body.

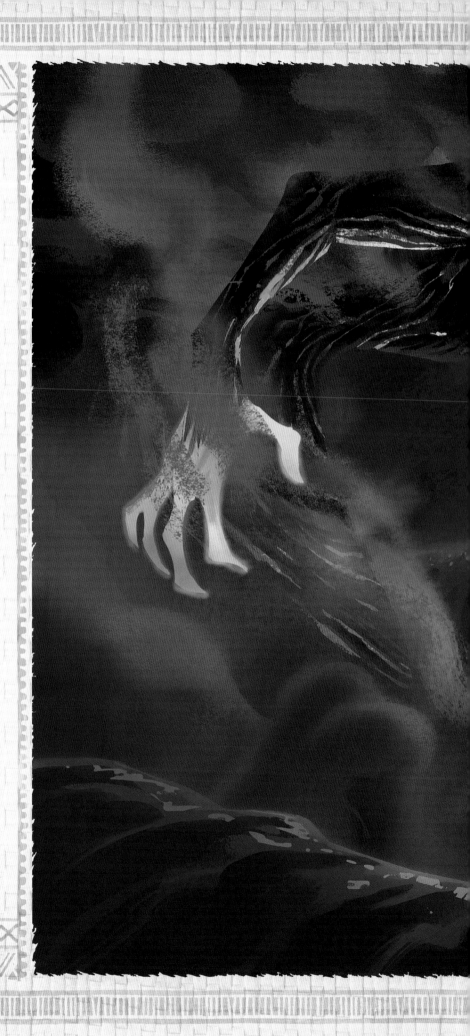

Moana watched as the face of the lava monster
transformed. Now that the goddess's heart was
restored, she was changing back to her true self.

A crown of flowers blossomed around Te Fiti's
head and she took her place in the water. Her island
exploded with green and came back to life at last.

Maui was amazed at Moana's bravery and so proud of his new friend. Te Fiti had forgiven Maui for taking her heart, and even fixed his fishhook for him!

Back on their boat, Maui and Moana prepared to go their separate ways. The new friends hugged before Maui shape-shifted into a hawk and flew away. But this wasn't goodbye – Moana knew that Maui would be there whenever she needed him.

Back on Motunui, Moana's parents were desperately worried about their missing daughter. They were overjoyed when she appeared on the horizon in her little boat.

Later that day, with a shell in her hand, Moana headed up the tallest mountain, to the pile of rocks her father had once shown her, and proudly added her shell to the top.

Moana finally knew who she was –
the next great ocean explorer, destined to
lead her people on amazing new adventures!